# Late for the Party

Alice Hemming

Illustrated by
Nick Roberts

"Hurry up and get dressed quickly,"
said Mum. "Lily's party starts at two
o'clock."

"Mum … " said Alfie.
"Not now," said Mum, "We don't want to be late. Tell me when you're dressed."

"Well done, Alfie. Now, what did you want to tell me?"

"I have to dress up," said Alfie. "It's a fancy dress party."

"Ah," said Mum. "You'd better get changed again."

"You look great," said Mum. "Now let's wrap the present quickly. We don't want to be late."

"Shoes on! Coat and gloves on!" said
Mum. "We need to leave
in two minutes."
"Mum … " said Alfie.

"Not now," said Mum. "We don't want to be late. Tell me on the way. Now shut the door and let me lock it."

"Well done, Alfie. Now what did you want to tell me?"

"The present is still on the table," said Alfie.

"Oh dear," said Mum. "Let's run home and get it."

"Off we go again," said Mum.
"We are late now. We will have
to run to get to the hall on time."

"Mum … " said Alfie.

"Not now," said Mum. "Tell me when we get there."

"We made it at last. Now what did you want to tell me?"
"The party is at Lily's house.
It's not at the hall," said Alfie.

"Oh no!" said Mum. "We must go back the other way! Hurry up! It's two o'clock now."

"Hello Lily. Happy birthday.
I'm sorry we're late for your party."

"You're not late," said Lily's mum.
"You're early. The party is not today
– it's tomorrow!"